Kitten Rescue

Lucy Daniels

With special thanks to Lucy Courtenay

ORCHARD BOOKS

First published in Great Britain in 2018 by The Watts Publishing Group

1 3 5 7 9 10 8 6 4 2

A CIP catalogue record for this book
is available from the British Library.

ISBN 978 1 40835 414 8

Printed and bound in Great Britain by CPI Group (UK) Ltd, Croydon, CR0 4YY
The paper and board used in this book are made from wood from responsible sources.

Orchard Books
An imprint of
Hachette Children's Group
Part of The Watts Publishing Group Limited
Carmelite House
50 Victoria Embankment
London EC4Y 0DZ

An Hachette UK Company
www.hachette.co.uk
www.hachettechildrens.co.uk

Kitten Rescue

CONTENTS

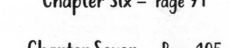

CHAPTER ONE

Amelia Haywood stared at the big pile of packing boxes in the corner of her new bedroom.

"I don't know where to start!" she said.

"Just take it slowly," said her mum. She opened one of the boxes and took out a pile of Amelia's favourite animal books.

"Here," she said, handing them to her.
"Why don't you start with these?"

Amelia took the books, but a sudden
rush of homesickness came over her.
She sat down on the bed with a sigh.

Mum sat next to her, putting her arm
around Amelia's shoulders. Her blue eyes,
the same shade as Amelia's own, were
warm. "It's all a bit strange, isn't it?" she
said softly. "But don't worry. We're going
to be very happy living here with Gran,
I promise."

"I know," said Amelia, doing her best not to sound too gloomy. "I'm fine, Mum. Honest. I'll unpack the rest of my things, OK?"

Her mum kissed the top of her head, then headed downstairs. Taking a deep breath, Amelia stacked the animal books neatly on the shelf above her bed. In her old house, there'd been a bookshelf by the door. She didn't want to think about her old, familiar bedroom, with its polka-dot wallpaper and glowing star stickers on the ceiling, but it was difficult. She liked some things about her new room – the seat built into the wall below the window, and the sloping ceiling.

But although she'd always loved coming here to visit Gran, it just wasn't home.

Amelia went through the boxes. Her games console went on the shelf beside her computer, with her magazines next to it. She put the tablet with its guinea pig cover in a drawer. But even with her things around her, the room still felt odd.

Amelia bit her lip. She'd left all her friends and everything she knew behind in York – even her dad, now he and her mum were divorced. *What's it going to be like*, she thought, *living here in Welford?* Would she make friends? And what about school? Term was due to start next week. Everything had changed so quickly.

Her eyes suddenly wet with tears, Amelia went to curl up on the window seat, hugging her knees to her chest. In the garden below, a blackbird was on the lawn, pecking for worms. There was a furry flash as a squirrel raced up a tree. And was that tiny rainbow gleam hovering over the garden pond a dragonfly? Despite everything,

Amelia felt a stir of excitement.

Animals always make me feel better, she thought, wiping her eyes. *And I've never lived anywhere with so many!* All she'd seen from their old flat in York was the side of another house and a row of blue dustbins.

Perhaps living here wouldn't be *all* bad. Downstairs, boxes of plates and bowls stood half-unpacked on the kitchen table, and a mixing bowl sat on the shining work surface. Amelia's mum was twisting the dials on the oven. "Eggs," she muttered to herself. "Why didn't I get some eggs?"

"What are you making, Mum?" Amelia asked.

Her mum sighed. "Salted caramel cupcakes," she said. "But we don't have any eggs!" Her face became sad, as if a cloud had blown across it. Amelia had seen that look several times since the divorce – she knew that her mum was upset about moving too.

"I get eggs from my friend Dervla just outside the village," said Amelia's grandmother, who was standing in the kitchen door. "Dervla keeps chickens, so they're

as fresh as you can get."

"Why don't I go and buy some?" Amelia suggested. It would give her mum one less thing to worry about – and maybe she'd see even more animals in the village. Ducks on the pond, maybe, or rabbits in the fields?

Mum ruffled Amelia's hair. "That's a lovely idea, but I'm afraid I haven't got time to come with you right now. There's still so much unpacking to do."

"That's one of the good things about living in the countryside," said Gran. "It's much safer than walking around a busy city like York. Amelia will be fine on her own as long as she's sensible."

Amelia's heart lifted. "I *will* be sensible –
I promise!"

Her gran quickly drew Amelia a map
on the back of an
envelope. "If you take
that road there," she
said, showing Amelia
with the tip of her
finger, "you'll reach

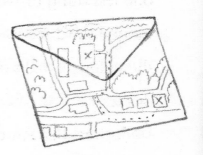

Dervla's farm in no time at all. Enjoy the
walk. And don't get lost!"

Amelia tucked the map into her back
pocket then headed outside. The sun
was warm on her face as she headed
up the street. She went past the bed and
breakfast sign and left at the bus stop,

then straight ahead at the village pond, with its fringe of spiky green reeds and two mallards quacking at each other. *This place is bigger than I expected*, she thought. She passed the Indian takeaway, checking that her favourite thing – coconut naan bread – was on the menu, and glanced into the newsagent's. They had lots of magazines, so she promised herself she'd come back and look properly another time.

According to Gran's map, she had to take the lane just after the Fox and Goose pub. She turned down the leafy little lane.

"*EGGS FOR SALE,*" said the sign

outside the farm gate. Amelia grinned. Striding up to the farmhouse door, she knocked. A lady with wispy black hair and large blue eyes opened the door.

"You must be Amelia," said the lady with a smile.

Amelia nodded, surprised. "How did you know?"

"Your gran called and told me to look out for you. I'm Dervla." She pressed a box of shiny brown eggs into Amelia's hands. "Half a dozen free-range eggs, laid this morning!"

"Thanks!" Amelia handed Dervla the money and put the eggs carefully in her backpack. "We'll save you a cupcake!"

she called, as she set off back to the road.

On the way home, she stopped to watch a farmer and his collie dog herding sheep in a field, and peered into a stable where a pony was being groomed. The sound of quacking made her look round. She grinned in delight – three more ducks were landing on the pond, wings flapping, webbed feet stretched out as they hit the water.

Amelia jumped down the steps that led to the road before remembering about the fragile eggs. *Oops!* She put down her backpack and opened up the carton, pleased to see that the eggs were still safe – then almost dropped them, as a tortoiseshell cat sprinted over the road in front of her in blur of white, brown and ginger.

"Wait!" Amelia called. But the cat scrambled over the wall that ran along the the far side of the road and vanished. *Was it wearing a collar?* Amelia wondered. She couldn't be sure, but she didn't think so. *Who does it belong to? And what was it running away from?*

"Woof! Woof!"
Amelia spun
around. An adorable
little Westie puppy
came rushing on to
the road, its little pink
tongue lolling.

It had short legs and a long face, and its
white fur curled at the ends. The puppy
was clearly chasing the cat, but when it
had scampered over the road and reached
the wall, it couldn't follow any further.
Instead it ran up and down on the road,
barking wildly up at the wall.

A dull rumbling sound was
approaching. *What now?* Amelia

wondered, spinning around. A car was coming down the country road towards her. Amelia gasped with horror. It was speeding towards the puppy! Her heart leaped into her mouth.

Without thinking, she ran into the road. She threw her arms in the air and the eggs went sailing from her hands, splattering on the pavement.

"Stop!" she screamed, then clamped her eyes shut.

CHAPTER TWO

Amelia cringed at the squeal of tyres. She opened her eyes and saw the car had stopped – just in time! The puppy stood frozen, with one paw in the air. Amelia ran round to the driver's window.

"Thank you!" she said breathlessly. "I was so worried you wouldn't see him."

The teenage girl in the driving seat
looked pale with shock. She pushed
back her dark blonde hair, unbuckled
her seatbelt and got out of the car.
The little Westie ran around in circles on
the tarmac, barking.

"Is the puppy yours?"
the girl asked. She
looked a little shaky.
Amelia shook
her head. "I was just
walking back to my gran's
when a cat ran into the road. The dog
was chasing her."

"Thank goodness you stopped me,"
said the girl. "We'd better catch him,

hadn't we? Before any more cars come along the road."

Amelia and the blonde girl approached the Westie slowly, but he skipped away from them and barked merrily. *He thinks it's a game*, Amelia realised. The puppy looked very young, and didn't respond when they told him to "sit" or "stay". He just barked, wagged his tail and darted out of the way. He wasn't wearing a collar, either, so Amelia tried to grab him around his tummy as he raced past. She almost got him, her hands closing around his soft, warm middle, but she skidded in the puddle of broken eggs and the dog slipped through her grasp.

"Lively, isn't he?" said the girl, wiping her forehead. "It'll be easier if we catch him by the scruff – the skin on the back of his neck. It's how mother dogs carry their puppies." She grinned. "I'm Mandy, by the way. Mandy Hope."

"Amelia Haywood," Amelia panted. "I've just moved to Welford with my mum. We're living with my gran now." She looked down to see if she'd got eggs on her dungaree shorts. *Ooh, I*

have an idea. Dabbling her
fingers in the broken
eggs, she held her hand.

"Come here, pup,"
she said in her most
encouraging voice.
"Yummy eggs."

The puppy came towards her with his
nose quivering. Closer and closer …

"Got you!" Amelia exclaimed, grasping
the puppy's scruff and lifting him up into
her arms. He was warm and wriggly
against her chest.

"Well done!" Mandy said as the puppy
licked Amelia's face. "That was really
quick thinking."

"Woof!" yipped the puppy, his stumpy little tail a blur. *He's adorable*, Amelia thought. *But so naughty!*

"There's no sign of the cat," she said, remembering the flash of tortoiseshell with a sudden stab of anxiety. "Do you think she's OK?"

"She's probably hiding quietly somewhere," Mandy replied. "Don't worry. Cats are good at finding their way home."

"There you are, Amelia!"

Amelia looked round to see her gran coming down the road, one hand shading her eyes.

"Your mum and I were wondering if

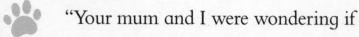

you'd got lost," she said. "Hello, Mandy."

"Colette!" said Mandy. "I'm guessing you're Amelia's grandmother?"

"Indeed I am," said her gran.

"Do you know each other?" said Amelia in surprise.

Her gran smiled. "Everyone knows everyone in Welford, darling. You'll soon learn that." She peered at the wriggling puppy in Amelia's arms. "Who have you got there?"

Amelia explained what had happened.

"He isn't wearing a collar," said Mandy, tickling the puppy's fat, furry tummy. "I'll take him to Animal Ark. Someone there will probably know who he belongs to."

"What's Animal Ark?" Amelia asked with interest, imagining a huge boat full of animals, bobbing on the Welford pond.

"Animal Ark is the vet's surgery here in Welford," Mandy explained. "My parents run it."

A vet's surgery! The image of a boat disappeared. In its place, Amelia pictured a brightly lit, modern surgery full of creatures in need.

"Woof! Woof!"

Amelia realised that she'd been squeezing the puppy a little too hard in her excitement. She kissed his head apologetically, then looked at Mandy and Gran. "Can I go too?" she begged.

"I've never been to a vet's surgery before."

"If it's OK with Mandy, then it's OK with me," her grandmother said.

"Of course you can come," said Mandy. "You'll love it. We'll drive there, it'll only take us five minutes."

Amelia suddenly remembered. "I'm sorry, Gran," she said, biting her lip, "but I dropped the eggs, and—"

"Then she used them to catch the puppy," finished Mandy with a grin.

"They've been good for something,

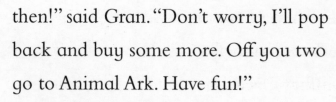

then!" said Gran. "Don't worry, I'll pop back and buy some more. Off you two go to Animal Ark. Have fun!"

Amelia climbed into the car, holding the squirming puppy on her lap. On the back seat was a suitcase and boxes filled with books and clothes.

"I'm on my way to university," Mandy explained, pulling her keys from her pocket. "I'm studying to be a vet, just like my parents."

"A vet!" Amelia looked at Mandy in awe. "That's amazing!"

As Mandy switched the engine on, the little Westie began to whine and scrabble around in Amelia's arms. Amelia cuddled

him close. It must be confusing to be in this strange place without anything familiar. *I know how you feel*, she thought, stroking his soft ears. "You poor thing," she said gently. "We'll find your owner really soon."

The puppy stopped whimpering and licked her hand. Amelia glanced at Mandy as they drove down a narrow lane with stone houses and brightly coloured flowers. *How amazing to look after animals all the time*, she thought. *Maybe I could be a vet one day too.*

The words "*ANIMAL ARK, VETERINARY SURGERY*" were painted on a wooden sign in bold, black

letters at the end of a drive. Amelia sat
up and gazed out of the window as
they swung in and stopped in a small
parking area. The surgery wasn't how
she'd imagined at all. Instead of the sleek,
modern building she'd pictured, Animal
Ark looked like a house: an ordinary
stone cottage, with beautiful geraniums
around the porch and three wide steps.

But then the doors opened, and out came a man with an enormous Great Dane, its tail wagging despite the bandage on its paw. A little boy and his mum held the door open for a lady holding a cat basket. In the boy's arms was a small mesh case with a white rabbit inside.

Amelia tingled with excitement. "So many animals!" she said.

Mandy grinned. "Just wait until you see inside."

Amelia followed Mandy up the steps and through the glass doors. This part of the surgery was *exactly* how she had imagined it.

The reception was bright and clean, full of people with pets on their laps, or by their feet. Amelia didn't know where to look first — she could see a Labrador with a plastic cone around its neck, several cats in their travel baskets, eyeing

each other through the bars, and two loudly squeaking guinea pigs. A lady sitting on the far side of the room had a blue parrot in a large cage by her feet.

A thrill shot through Amelia. *This is the best place ever!*

CHAPTER THREE

"I've never seen *so many animals* in one place!" Amelia said. She couldn't stop staring at them. A woman had a plastic box lined with sand on her knees, a small green gecko inside. A sausage dog was chewing a toy beneath a chair.

"I know, isn't it brilliant?" Mandy's eyes

shone. "I'm going to miss Animal Ark so much when I'm at uni. Come on, I'll introduce you to everyone."

The Westie puppy stretched up and licked Amelia's nose. Amelia cuddled him closer as she followed Mandy to the reception desk, but he yipped and squirmed, trying to pull away from her arms. He was staring at a black cat in a blue plastic travel basket.

"Back already, Mandy?" asked the lady on reception, who was in a wheelchair. She smiled at Amelia.

"I know!" said Mandy. "I can never leave an animal in trouble. Amelia, this is Julia Kaminski. Julia, meet Amelia, puppy

rescuer extraordinaire. She's new to
the village."

Julia tucked her dark hair behind her
ears. "Welcome to Welford, Amelia,"
she said. "That pup is quite a handful,
isn't he?"

"Definitely," said Amelia, a little out of
breath.

Mandy knocked on a door to one
side of the reception desk. "Simon?" she
called. "It's me. Can I come in?"

"Bored of uni already?" came the reply.

Amelia followed Mandy into a small
room with a little window set high up.
A man was struggling with something
large and fluffy on a set of scales in the

middle of a table. Amelia glimpsed a pair of bright eyes and a twitching nose, and two long floppy ears.

"Is that a French Lop rabbit?" she asked, entranced.

The man blew his hair out of his eyes as he got a firmer grip on the fluffball. "Blossom here is indeed a French Lop," he said. "She weighs six kilos. What *have* you been eating, Blossom?"

"Simon is our veterinary nurse,"

Mandy explained. "He gets all the fun jobs around here."

Amelia wanted to stroke Blossom, but didn't dare let go of the little dog in her arms – he was sniffing the rabbit with great interest. Mandy ushered her back out, pointing out different areas of the surgery.

"All our supplies are kept in there," she explained, showing Amelia a room behind the reception desk. "And through here, you'll find our hotel."

"Hotel?" said Amelia in surprise, picturing rooms with big beds and fluffy white towels.

Mandy laughed. "Sometimes we need

to keep animals in overnight. This is
where they stay."

She held open the door so that Amelia
could look inside. The rows of cages
on the back wall had two occupants: a
cat with a bandage on her tail, and a
hamster half-hidden in sawdust, with
what looked like a splint on its back leg.
The cat blinked sleepily at Amelia with
large green eyes.

Amelia turned to see two vets
emerging from the consulting rooms.
They both wore green scrubs – loose-
fitting tops and trousers – and matching
expressions of surprise.

"Hi, Mum, hi, Dad," Mandy said.
"This is Amelia. We don't know what the
puppy's called. We found him loose in the
road without a collar."

"Typical," said Mrs Hope, laughing.
"We only sent you to university an hour
ago and already you're back with an
animal in distress."

Mr Hope smiled at Amelia. "Did
Mandy rescue you as well?"

"I guess she did," said Amelia, her

cheeks flushing. She suddenly felt shy. "I'm new in Welford."

"I started helping out at Animal Ark when I was around your age," Mandy told Amelia.

"That's true." Mrs Hope stroked the little Westie between the ears. She smiled at her daughter. "It's already very strange without you, love."

Amelia's heart beat faster. She gazed longingly at the animal posters on the walls and the dog-walking leaflets on the pinboard. Should she ask? It had to be worth a try …

"Maybe I could help out instead?" she blurted. "I mean, while Mandy's away. It would be amazing to spend time here with all the animals."

Mr and Mrs Hope glanced at each other. Their expressions were uncertain.

"Well," said Mrs Hope slowly, "it's so nice of you to offer. But helping at a vet's is much harder than people think."

Mr Hope nodded. "It's not just cute puppies, I'm afraid," he said. "Lots of the animals we see are really sick. Taking care of them is hard work."

"Maybe when you're older," said Mrs Hope. "But it's too much responsibility right now."

Amelia felt like a bubble had burst somewhere within her. "Oh," she said. "Maybe one day, then."

"Come on, pup," said Mandy, lifting the Westie gently from Amelia's arms. "Let's find out who you are."

Amelia followed the older girl into a consulting room. Mandy put the puppy on the rubber-covered examining table in the centre and opened a cabinet. She took out a handheld device with a

digital screen. "It's a microchip scanner,"
she told Amelia. Mandy moved the
little device around the Westie's body,
hovering around his neck and back. The
scanner let out a beep.

"Aha!" Mandy said, examining the
little screen. "He's got a chip."

"What does it say?" asked Amelia
eagerly, craning her neck.

Mandy showed her a long string of numbers. "Just need to look it up on the website," she said, turning to the computer and starting to type. After a few moments, she said, "Here he is. His name's Mac."

"Woof!" said the puppy, pricking up his white ears.

"Yes, that's you!" Amelia said, ruffling the dog's soft fur. "So who do you belong to, Mac?"

"*Baxter*," read Mandy. "The Baxters run the bed and breakfast in the village. Their number's with Mac's information." She reached for the phone then called the number. Mandy explained what had happened, and Amelia heard a cry of delight on the other end of the line. "He's fine," said Mandy. "Yes, we understand. No problem, Mrs Baxter, we can look after Mac here. Great. Bye." She hung up. "They've got new guests arriving in a bit, so they can't collect Mac yet. You'll have to stay here for a couple of hours, boy."

As the puppy whimpered, Amelia felt a rush of sympathy. He was missing his owners, she could tell.

"Where do the Baxters live?" she asked.

"Around fifteen minutes' walk from here," said Mrs Hope. She and Mr Hope had joined them in the consulting room.

An idea came to Amelia. She felt a burst of courage. *This is my chance!* she thought. *I'll prove to the Hopes that I can help out here!*

"Why don't I walk him home?" she suggested.

Mr and Mrs Hope looked at each other again. This time they seemed pleased.

"Good idea," said Mrs Hope. "We're pretty busy in here today."

"I'll show you the way," offered Mandy. "It doesn't matter if I get to uni a bit late."

Mr Hope popped into the supplies room and came out with a red collar and lead. "Mac can borrow these," he suggested. "The Baxters can bring them back later."

Mac stayed perfectly still as Amelia carefully fitted the collar around his furry neck. *It's as if he knows he's going home,* Amelia thought. She clipped on the lead and set him down on the floor.

"Come on then, Mac," she said as Mandy held open the door. "Walkies!"

The pair of them set off, Mac trotting ahead. He tugged on the lead, pulling Amelia back down the Animal Ark driveway. His tail waved happily from side to side as he sniffed the pavement.

"It feels like he's the one taking me for a walk," said Amelia, breaking into a jog to keep up with the puppy.

"Mac! Heel!" called Mandy.

But Mac ignored her. Amelia felt as
if her arm was being pulled out of its
socket. In York she'd walked her auntie's
elderly Yorkshire terriers, but Mac wasn't
anything like them – he was in a rush,
sniffing everywhere, scampering from
side to side. His tail was a blur as they
approached the end of the lane, his nose
pressed hard to the pavement.

"I think he's picked up a scent," said
Mandy, as Mac's tail wagged even more
madly. "Why don't I take the lead for a
while?"

"No, it's fine," Amelia began. "I can
handle—"

Mac lunged forward. The lead slithered
out of Amelia's grip.

"Oh!" she cried in dismay as the puppy
shot off down the lane. "Mac! MAC!
Come back!"

Her heart plummeted. If Mac got lost
again, it would be her fault!

CHAPTER FOUR

Amelia chased after the puppy, Mandy running alongside. Her heart was thumping like a drum and she stumbled over clumps of weeds and potholes. What if a car came around the corner again, and she couldn't stop it this time? She would never forgive herself if Mac got hurt.

When she reached the corner of the road, she looked wildly left and right. There were no cars – just a bicycle, approaching fast.

And Mac was racing towards it.

"Watch out!" Amelia shouted, waving her arms.

"Stop!" cried Mandy. "The dog!"

The bike's front wheel wobbled as Mac pelted towards it. Curly black hair peeped out from beneath the cyclist's silver helmet. Amelia could hardly look as the bike swerved to a halt and the rider jumped off. It was a boy around the same age as Amelia.

The boy crouched down and stretched

out his arms. "Mac!" he cried, spluttering
as the puppy covered his face in licks.
"I've been so worried about you!"

"Woof!" yapped Mac, beside himself
with delight.

The cyclist pulled his helmet off.
Amelia drew a huge breath of relief, and
rested her hands on her knees.

"Hi!" said the boy with a friendly
smile. "I'm Sam –
Sam Baxter. Mum
said Animal Ark
called to say you'd
found Mac! Where
was the little guy?"

"Amelia found

him chasing a cat," Mandy explained breathlessly.

"I was about to give him a bath in the garden," Sam explained, "and as soon as I took off his collar he spotted a cat sitting on the wall. Off he ran!" He shook his head. "I couldn't catch him. I was really worried that without his collar no one would know who he was."

"You've got him back safely now," Mandy said with a grin.

Amelia tried to smile too, but the thought of giving Mac back made a lump form in her throat. *Don't be silly*, she told herself. *He's Sam's dog.* But still, she really wished she could spend time

with the adorable puppy again.

"We checked his microchip at the surgery," she said.

Sam's face cleared. "I'd forgotten about his chip. Cool!"

Mac started whining, and scampering around Amelia's feet. Amelia knelt down and stroked his ears.

"Don't apologise to me, Mac," she said as the puppy licked her hand. "Apologise to Sam!"

Mac cocked his head and looked at Sam. "Woof," he said, as if he really was saying sorry.

Sam burst out laughing. Amelia couldn't help joining in.

"He likes you," said Sam, grinning.
"Do you want to come back to my
house and play with him for a while?"

"Really?" Amelia said. "I'd love that!"

"I'd better head back to the surgery
and fetch my car," said Mandy, as Sam
produced Mac's collar and lead from his
backpack and swapped them for the red
ones. "Bye, Amelia. I think you're going

to really like living in Welford."

Amelia waved as the older girl walked back down the lane towards the surgery. *I hope she's right*, she thought.

"Come on, then," said Sam, tying Mac's lead to his handlebars. "It's not far."

Sam wheeled his bike, Mac trotting on one side, and Amelia walking on the other. They walked back through the village, following the path next to the river. A couple of runners passed them, but it was otherwise peaceful. Insects darted above the water and a heron dipped its long beak into the shallows.

"How long have you lived in Welford?" Amelia asked.

"For ever," said Sam. "What about you?"

"I just moved here with my mum," Amelia explained. "We're living with my gran in the village now."

"Where did you live before?"

"We had a flat in York, right in the city centre," Amelia said. "There was a restaurant downstairs and shops over the road."

"Bit different to here then," said Sam cheerfully.

Amelia laughed. "Definitely! And it does feel a bit … well, strange without my dad. He's still living in York. My parents are divorced now."

"Do you miss your dad?" asked Sam.

Amelia lifted her shoulders. "I'll see him at weekends," she said, "but yes. It's weird without him."

"It's a bit weird at the B&B sometimes too," Sam said. "Mum and Dad are really busy all the time, so I'm by myself a lot. That's why they let me get Mac, so I'd have some company."

"Lucky you," said Amelia wistfully. "I'd love to have a pet. Either a dog or a cat,

I like both. I wonder who that cat Mac chased belonged to? I hope she's OK."

"Me too," agreed Sam.

They turned down a lane, past a sign that creaked lightly in the breeze as it swung from two chains: "*THE OLD MILL BED AND BREAKFAST*". Amelia had seen the sign before, just that morning. She suddenly realised where they were.

"Oh!" she said in surprise. "I live really close to here. We're just down the next road."

"Cool!" said Sam. Mac wagged his tail. "That's right, Mac, we're nearly home."

The Old Mill lived up to its name.

It was a higgledy-piggledy building set right on the water, with uneven windows and a yellow front door. A large waterwheel churned up the river, with green farmland on the other side.

Sam set his bike against the side of the mill and untied Mac's lead. The puppy was already pulling towards the door. From inside came a raised voice.

"This really is the last time!"

"Uh-oh," muttered Sam.

They slipped through the front door. A woman stood in the hallway with a bald man in motorbike leathers. The deep frown lines on the man's shiny pink forehead made him look like a grumpy bulldog. The woman wore a flowery blouse and trousers, and had the same bright eyes and curly hair as Sam. She had a worried look on her face.

The man waved a mangled boot in the air. "Look at the state of it!" he shouted. "This is the third one that your puppy has ruined already."

"I'm so sorry, Mr Ferguson," said the woman – Mrs Baxter, Amelia realised. "Mac is very young. We're doing all we can to train him, but—"

"Train him harder or get rid of him!" boomed Mr Ferguson. "I can't afford to buy a new pair of boots every week!"

"Mr Ferguson stays here a lot," Sam whispered. "He has business meetings nearby. He's always complaining about Mac, but he likes Dad's breakfasts so much that he always comes back."

Mac yapped. Mr Ferguson turned at the noise and scowled. The lines on his forehead became even deeper.

"That puppy," he said, "is a menace."

He stomped upstairs. The paintings on the walls shook as he slammed a door. Mrs Baxter sighed.

"Mum?" said Sam. "This is Amelia."

"Hello, Amelia," said Mrs Baxter, then looked sharply at Sam. "Promise me that you'll do something about Mac's training, won't you? We can't afford to lose Mr Ferguson's business."

"I will," said Sam, looking down at his trainers. "I promise."

"Your dad and I wish we could help, but we just don't have time. There are the breakfasts to make, and the beds to change, and the washing to do ..."

"I get it, Mum," Sam interrupted. "I'm

sorry, OK? I promise I'll train him."

Mac had trotted over to a chair in the hallway and was sniffing around its wooden legs.

"Um," Amelia began, "I think Mac is going to—"

The puppy lifted his fluffy leg and peed against the chair. The puddle spread, darkening the carpet.

"Mac, no!" shouted Sam in dismay. Mac jumped around his feet, yapping gleefully and looking pleased with himself.

"Not again! You're supposed to do that in the garden!"

71

"Oh, Mac!" Mrs Baxter cried. "This is all we need! Sam, if Mac's behaviour doesn't improve, we're going to have to give him up. I'm sorry, but we won't have a choice. We can't run a B&B like this."

A door opened. Through it, Amelia could see a big kitchen, the worktop stacked with dishes. A man with messy brown hair and a stubbly beard came out. "Another mess?" he said, holding up a cloth and a spray-bottle of disinfectant. "I'll deal with it, love," he said to Mrs Baxter. "Hi, Sam. Who's your friend?"

"Dad, this is Amelia," said Sam.

"Welcome to the madhouse, Amelia."
Mr Baxter laughed, kneeling down to
scrub at the mess on the
carpet.

A set of tyres crunched on
gravel outside. Through
the window, Amelia saw a
car with suitcases tied to
the roof rack. Mrs Baxter
went outside to greet the
new guests while Mr Baxter scooped up
the cloth and vanished back into
the kitchen. Sam stroked Mac's little
white ears.

"I can't lose you, Mac," he muttered to
the puppy, his shoulders slumped. "You've

got to stop being so naughty."

Amelia felt a tug of sympathy as she watched Sam pick up the little puppy. Mac licked his face. *I've got to make sure they stay together!* Amelia thought.

"I'm sure Mac will learn how to behave," Amelia said to Sam. "Why don't I help you train him?"

Sam's face brightened. "Really?"

Amelia had never trained a dog before, but she felt sure that she could work it out. She glanced at Mac, who blinked up at her, his fluffy ears pricked.

"We'll do it together," she promised. "How hard can it be?"

CHAPTER FIVE

"Of course you can stay out." Amelia
could hear the smile in her mum's voice.
"I'm so pleased you've made a friend!
Your gran says the Baxters are a lovely
family. Don't worry, the cupcakes
can wait."

"Thanks, Mum! Bye!" Amelia put the

phone back on the B&B's reception desk and went back to join Sam and Mac in the lounge.

"Sit," Sam was saying. "Mac, SIT!"

The puppy ran under the sofa. Amelia could see his stumpy little tail wagging.

"What am I doing wrong?" said Sam. "He won't listen to me *at all*."

"We just need some help," Amelia said. "Do you think your parents would let us use their computer?"

A few minutes later, they were sitting in the B&B's office in front of the computer screen. Amelia typed "Dog training video" into the search engine. Soon, a chirpy lady was on the screen, a large Alsatian at her side. "*Praise your dog when he does something right!*" she said, as the big dog panted happily. "*Good boy, Danny!*"

"But we have to get Mac to *do* something right first," Sam pointed out. "And how are we going to do that?"

Amelia thought back to Mac peeing on the chair in reception. She typed "Dog toilet training" and scanned through a couple of articles.

"This one says you mustn't make a fuss when your dog pees indoors," she said, pointing at the screen. "Instead you're supposed to give them praise when they pee outside. It says that dogs love getting attention, even if it's for bad behaviour."

"We always shout at Mac when he pees inside," Sam admitted. "Maybe it just makes it worse."

Amelia nodded. "Do you have any dog treats we can use as rewards?"

Sam went to the kitchen and came back with a small bag of treats. In the lounge, Amelia tipped out one of the chewy biscuits and held it towards the sofa where Mac was hiding. "Look, Mac!"

Mac's nose twitched. He wriggled out from his hiding place and took the treat. Amelia giggled at the feel of his damp nose and tickly fur. The puppy swallowed the biscuit – then started walking around in a circle, sniffing at the curtains.

"Uh oh – I think he's going to pee again!" said Amelia.

Sam rushed to scoop Mac up, and they hurried outside into the sunny garden. As soon as Sam put Mac down, he lifted his leg against a rose bush.

"Quick, praise him!" Amelia squealed.

"Clever boy, Mac!" cried Sam when the puppy had finished.

"Well done, Mac!" said Amelia, giving

the puppy's soft, furry tummy a rub.

Sam gave Mac another treat to reward him. "That was good. But how do we make him remember what to do?"

"The video said you have to do it over and over again," Amelia said. "Then he'll learn."

"Sounds like fun," said Sam with a grin.

Mac started zigzagging around the grass, sniffing. He dashed towards the garage and sniffed hard at the garage door. Amelia and Sam watched in surprise. The Westie barked and wagged his tail.

"What's in the garage?" Amelia asked.

"Just gardening stuff and Mr Ferguson's

motorbike," said Sam with a frown.
"I wonder what Mac can smell?"

"Maybe it's mice," suggested Amelia.
"Or maybe a bird's got stuck in there.
Come on, let's find out. But we'd
better put Mac inside in case he scares
whatever it is."

After Sam had put the wriggling
puppy indoors, they opened the heavy
garage door and peered inside. The
garage was gloomy, lit only by a small,
half-open window. Amelia could see the
gleam of Mr Ferguson's motorbike. There
was a stack of oil cans to one side, and
boxes of screws, hammers and paint pots
lined the shelves on the walls. A bundle

of gardening forks and spades leaned against the back wall. And somewhere in the middle of it all, something was squeaking.

"Can you hear that?" whispered Amelia.

Sam nodded, his eyes wide.

They crept inside. Amelia looked behind the motorbike while Sam checked out the shelves. The squeaking grew louder as they approached the gardening equipment. A leather biker jacket was lying on the concrete floor, and nestled on top of the jacket …

"Oh!" gasped Amelia.

Four tiny kittens lay curled up together.

They were so small that their ears still lay close to their heads and their eyes were closed. They could only have been a few days old.

"Kittens!" Sam sounded dazed. "What are they doing on Mr Ferguson's jacket?"

One kitten was ginger, and the other three were tortoiseshell. *Tortoiseshell* ... Amelia remembered the cat that Mac had chased earlier. She had been a tortoiseshell – and Amelia knew that

tortoiseshells weren't very common.

And now that she thought about it, she'd seen the cat running from the direction of the B&B ...

Suddenly the pieces fitted together like a jigsaw. "The mother cat must be the one Mac was chasing!" she said aloud. "She must have been here. That's why Mac ran off when you were giving him a bath – he saw her and chased after her."

The kittens really were tiny. They were mewing softly, kneading the air with their paws. Their little mouths were open.

"I think they're hungry," said Sam anxiously.

Amelia nodded. She felt a twist of

worry inside. *If they don't get food, they might die.*

"I think we should call Animal Ark," she said, "and ask them for advice."

Amelia and Sam sprinted back into the B&B and through to the kitchen, where Mac lay sound asleep in his basket. Sam's dad looked up from loading the dishwasher.

"Can we use your phone, Dad?" Sam asked, panting for breath. "We've found some kittens in the garage!"

Mr Baxter looked startled. "Of course you can. Are the kittens all right?" He took his phone from his pocket and passed it to Sam.

"We're not sure," Amelia said, as Sam called the number. He switched on the speaker button so Amelia could hear too.

"They sound like newborns," Mrs Hope said after Sam had explained. She sounded concerned. "They should be fed at least every two hours. How long is it since Mac chased the mother cat away, do you think?"

Amelia glanced at the clock on the kitchen wall. Her stomach flipped. "About two hours," she said.

Mrs Hope drew in a deep breath, and the knot in Amelia's stomach tightened. "They need urgent care if they're going to survive," the vet said. "Can you bring

86

them into Animal Ark right away? But you mustn't touch them – it's very important that you don't. If they smell of a strange scent it might stop the mother from bonding with them."

"I'll drive you," offered Mr Baxter, who was listening beside them. "Work can wait – these kittens are much more important!"

Sam ran to a cupboard and took out a cardboard box filled with video games. He tipped them out. Then they hurried back to the garage, where Mr Baxter helped them lift up the jacket and the kittens, being very careful not to touch them. The kittens' feeble mews broke Amelia's heart. She really wanted to

stroke them and make them feel better, but she couldn't risk it. It would be awful if the mother cat didn't want the kittens because of her.

Mr Ferguson came out of the house just as Sam, Amelia and Mr Baxter were hurrying to the car. Amelia was holding the box of kittens. One of the jacket's sleeves hung over the side, and when he spotted it, Mr Ferguson scowled.

"Don't tell me that puppy has chewed my jacket as well!" he snapped. "Of all the—"

"It's all right, Mr Ferguson," Mr Baxter said quickly, unlocking the car. "We'll bring your jacket back as soon as we've

taken these kittens to Animal Ark."

Mr Ferguson's eyebrows shot up.
"Kittens?" He peered into the box.

The kittens squeaked and wriggled on
the folds of the jacket. Amelia thought Mr
Ferguson's fierce expression grew softer as
he gazed at them.

"Kittens in my jacket!" he said. "I guess
it's an improvement on a puppy." He
waved a big hairy hand. "No rush, no
rush. Keep it as long as you need."

They got into the car, Amelia holding
the box on her knees. As Mr Baxter
drove off, Amelia glanced back to see
Mr Ferguson still standing in the drive,
watching the car.

"I think he liked the kittens," she said.

"He liked them better than he likes Mac," Sam replied gloomily. "That's for sure. Do you think the ginger one is OK?"

Amelia glanced into the box. The three tortoiseshell kittens were still mewing, but the ginger one was silent, lying on its side and hardly moving. Her heart raced with worry.

Are we too late?

CHAPTER SIX

While Mr Baxter parked, Amelia and
Sam carried the box of kittens into the
surgery together, taking extra care on
the steps. Though the reception area
was still busy, Julia waved them straight
through into one of the consultation
rooms, where Mrs Hope was holding
open the door.

"The first thing we need to do is warm the kittens up," said Mrs Hope, as Sam and Amelia carried the box inside. "Usually the heat from their mum's body would do that, but we'll have to use an incubator. Mr Hope's been called away to deal with a swan tangled in a fishing line, so would you like to help instead?"

Excitement rushed through Amelia – she couldn't quite believe this was happening. Sam was grinning beside her. "We'd love to help," Amelia said. "That would be brilliant."

Mrs Hope put on plastic gloves and lifted each kitten from the jacket, checking them over before placing them

into the incubator. Then she showed
Amelia and Sam how to mix up some
formula milk designed specially for
kittens.

"Then we heat it," she explained, "and
put it into these bottles."

Amelia helped to fill and seal the tiny
bottles with their soft rubber teats. Every
now and again, as she and Sam worked,

she glanced at the incubator and bit her lip. Mrs Hope gave Amelia and Sam gloves to wear too, so they wouldn't transfer their scent on to the kittens, then she passed them a kitten each. Sam got one of the tortoiseshells, Amelia carefully held the tiny ginger one, and Mrs Hope kept the other two tortoiseshells.

The kitten in Amelia's hand felt light as a feather. Its fur was as soft as a feather too, and when it gripped her fingers, its claws were like tiny needles. A rush of wonder and amazement filled Amelia, so strong she could hardly breathe.

"It's a boy," Mrs Hope explained, showing Amelia how to hold it. "Ginger cats are almost always boys. And tortoiseshells tend to be girls. We've posted a message online, by the way, asking if anyone has lost a cat."

"Have you had any replies?" Amelia asked hopefully.

Mrs Hope shook her head. "But it's early days."

They all held the bottles of milk close to the kittens' tiny mouths. The three tortoiseshells stirred and started sucking, pulling at the little teats hungrily until milk spattered their whiskers. Amelia let out a breath she didn't know she'd been holding. Then she looked down at the ginger kitten in her hands. His tiny mouth was turned away from the teat.

"Come on," she whispered. "Your sisters are doing it. You can do it too."

But the kitten didn't even seem to have the strength to lift his head.

Sam was watching the ginger kitten too. "I feel terrible," he mumbled. "If I'd trained Mac properly, he wouldn't have run off and chased the mother, and these kittens wouldn't even be here …"

"You didn't know what would happen," Amelia said, trying to keep her voice steady.

"You mustn't blame yourself," added

Mrs Hope. She took the bottle from
Amelia and nudged the ginger kitten's
mouth with the tip of the teat. The
kitten twitched. Mrs Hope pressed the
teat against its mouth again. The kitten's
whiskers trembled as its
mouth opened. Finally,
it began to feed. Amelia
grinned with relief. Mrs
Hope handed her the
bottle and she held it as
the kitten sucked. She
was feeding a kitten!

"You brought them
to us just in time," said Mrs Hope. "The
little ginger one is going to need lots

of help but – fingers crossed! – it looks hopeful that they will all survive."

By the time the kittens had emptied their bottles and were curled up in the warm incubator, the sky was getting dark outside the surgery windows. Amelia couldn't believe how quickly the day had passed.

There was a commotion in the reception area: the sound of the glass doors banging open and loud voices.

"Emily," said the receptionist, wheeling up to the door. "A large dog has just been brought in – it was hit by a tractor. Adam still isn't back, so could you … ?"

"Of course," said Mrs Hope, stripping

off her gloves and washing her hands at the sink. "Simon? Simon!"

The door swung open from the supplies room. "Already on it," said Simon, his arms full of bandages as he rushed through the surgery to one of the operating rooms.

Sam turned to Amelia. His eyes were wide. "No one's got time to look after the kittens now – and Mrs Hope said they would need feeding again in a couple of hours."

An idea floated through Amelia's head. More than anything in the world, she wanted to help out at Animal Ark all the time. This was another chance to show the Hopes just how helpful she could be.

"Don't worry," she said. "I've got a plan …"

"Amelia? Are you awake, love?"

Amelia rubbed her eyes. The clock on her bedside table glowed in the darkness – it said the time was one o'clock in the morning. In the pale light, Amelia saw her mum perched on the edge of the bed. Why had Mum woken her up? Then it all came rushing back. *Of course!* she realised. *It's time to feed the kittens again!*

The injured dog brought into Animal Ark had needed an operation, so while

Mrs Hope and Simon took care of it,
Mum and Gran had come over to fetch
Amelia and the kittens. Now the kittens
were sleeping in the lounge, on a special
heat pad borrowed from Animal Ark.
This was Amelia's first night in her new
home, and she'd been worried about
how she would feel sleeping in a strange
bed. But there was no time for her to be
homesick now. *Not while I've got the kittens
to look after!*

Pulling on her dressing gown and
slippers, Amelia padded down the stairs
after her mum. Gran was already in the
kitchen, mixing the formula and heating
it up in the tiny bottles. Yawning, but

determined to do it right, Amelia put on the special gloves and took the bottles into the lounge.

Amelia settled the ginger kitten on her lap and tucked the teat into his mouth. He didn't take much milk, but he seemed a little better than before. Mum and Gran did the same with the three tortoiseshell kittens. The clock ticked quietly on the mantelpiece. Amelia's

eyelids were heavy, threatening to droop.
Luckily school didn't start until next
week, as she knew she'd be tired in the
morning. But the sound of the ginger
kitten purring happily in her lap made
her sit up straight. *He's relying on me …*

Amelia had never looked after a
pet before, and was surprised by how
worrying it was – and how lovely.
*I guess Sam feels like this every day, looking
after Mac.*

"Good night!" Amelia said to Mum
and Gran, once the feeding was over
and the kittens were settled back on
the heat pad. "See you in two hours
for the next feed!"

"Why don't you let Gran and me do it," said Mum, "so you can sleep?"

Amelia shook her head. "Thanks, Mum," she said. "But I really want to look after them."

Back in her bedroom, she sat on the window seat to take off her slippers. Through a gap in the curtains she could just see the outline of the B&B, glowing against the moonlit sky. There was a light on in one of the windows.

Sleepily, she settled back under her duvet. *Maybe Sam's awake, worrying about the kittens too*, she thought. It was comforting that he was near. *I just hope they'll be all right …*

CHAPTER SEVEN

The doorbell rang at seven o'clock the next morning. Amelia opened the door to find Sam and Mac outside.

"Hello," she said through a yawn.

"I've come to see the kittens," said Sam. "Are they OK?"

Amelia rubbed her eyes. "Come see."

Sam tied Mac up outside and followed Amelia to the lounge. Amelia's grandmother was sitting on the sofa with the ginger kitten feeding from a bottle. Her mum sat by the window with one of the tortoiseshell kittens.

"The ginger one is feeding!" said Sam in delight.

"I know, isn't it great?" Amelia felt light-headed with exhaustion and pride. "He's doing loads better this morning. Gran, you know Sam, don't you? Sam, this is my mum."

"It's all go in here, Sam," said Mum. "Do you want to feed a kitten?"

Sam grinned. "Really? Cool!"

In the kitchen,
Amelia mixed more
formula and told Sam
what had happened
overnight. "Have
you seen the
mother cat?"
she asked.

Sam shook his head.
"I'm worried that she
won't come back."

"Then I think we'd better look for her,"
said Amelia, filling up the bottles.

Once the kittens were fed, Amelia
headed back to the B&B with Sam and
Mac. The puppy behaved well on his

lead as they strode along, not objecting when Sam pulled him away from sniffing the verge. And when he lifted his leg on a bush by the roadside, Sam was ready with a treat.

"Good boy!" Sam said, rubbing Mac's head. "He peed on the kitchen floor earlier," he told Amelia, "but I did what you suggested and I didn't make a fuss at all. I think he's learning."

"Of course he is!" said Amelia, stroking Mac too. "That video said that puppies want to please people – they just need to learn how!"

Back at the B&B, Sam shut Mac in the kitchen and he and Amelia headed

into the garden to look for clues about where the mother cat could be. They hunted under the bushes and along the riverbank, behind the shed and in the flowerbeds. Amelia remembered Mrs Hope's online post about the missing cat, and wondered if there had been any replies. *I'll call Animal Ark as soon as I get back home*, she decided.

Her eyes settled on something black and ginger fluttering on the wire fence between Sam's house and the farm next door.

"Sam!" she called. "Come and check this out!"

Sam climbed out of a flowerbed and

brushed the dirt from his knees.

"A tuft of fur!" he exclaimed. "Do you think it belongs to the cat?"

Amelia pulled the tuft from the fence and examined it more closely. "It's multi-coloured like a tortoiseshell ..."

"That's Spring Farm," said Sam, nodding over the fence. "Mr Stevens is the farmer. He's nice."

"Maybe the mother cat visits the farm," said Amelia. "There are probably lots of mice in his barns."

Sam looked excited. "Let's go and ask Mr Stevens if he's seen her."

After they'd told Mrs Baxter where they were going, and left Mac snoozing in his basket, Amelia and Sam headed to Spring Farm, taking with them a tin of tuna and an old cat carry basket Sam had found in the shed. Amelia pushed open the farm's gate, taking care  to shut it behind her so that none of the animals could get out.

Spring Farm had several huge barns and a large field full of grazing cows. A new barn was halfway through being built, and there was a lot of noise as

builders hammered, sawed and called instructions to each other.

"This place is huge," Amelia said, her heart sinking as she gazed around.

Sam cupped his hand to his ear. "Eh? What was that?"

Amelia raised her voice over the builders' noise. "I said, the farm's huge! How will we find the cat here?"

Sam pointed at the farmhouse, a white building with a mud-spattered car parked outside. "Let's start there," he shouted back.

They headed over and knocked. A man with grey stubble on his tanned cheeks, and lots of lines around his eyes, opened the door. He pushed back his cap and gazed inquiringly at Sam and Amelia.

"Hi, Mr Stevens," said Sam. "This is my friend Amelia. We're looking for a missing cat – have you seen her?"

Mr Stevens looked thoughtful. "What does she look like?"

"She has tortoiseshell fur," Amelia said. "And she's skinny, with white paws."

"She's got four kittens," Sam said. "We want to find her so she can look after them."

Mr Stevens nodded. "I've seen a cat like that. She seems scared of people, though. I've tried to pet her but she won't let me come very close."

For the first time, Amelia wondered if
the tortoiseshell cat might not have an
owner at all.

"But I didn't know about the kittens,"
Mr Stevens went on. "I haven't seen her
recently, but I can show you where she
usually is."

Amelia and Sam hurried after the

farmer as he strode towards the barns. The builders had started up their machinery again, and the air hummed with noise. One of them was driving a forklift truck loaded with timber.

"I read somewhere that cats like to give birth to their kittens somewhere quiet," Amelia shouted over the noise as they entered the first barn. It was dark and musty, with bales of hay scattered around. "Maybe all the building work scared her away to Sam's garage?"

Mr Stevens nodded. "It's certainly been noisy around here lately." He pointed at the hay bales. "This is where she likes to sleep. Be careful, though – the bales are heavy, so don't try to move them."

He left them to it. Sam opened the cat basket and placed the tuna inside. He and Amelia set it down on top of a bale of hay, then hid behind another pile of bales and waited. Amelia's pulse was racing, and it was difficult to sit still with the hay prickling through her clothes. She could feel how tense Sam was as he sat beside her. *I really hope the mother cat is here ...*

After what felt like hours, Amelia was close to falling asleep. The long night of feeding the kittens had left her very tired – but she'd definitely do it again! Then Sam nudged her arm, and pointed.

A shadow emerged from a dusty corner. Amelia couldn't help but gasp. The tortoiseshell cat looked thinner than she remembered. It moved cautiously through the hay bales towards the basket, its whiskers twitching. *Just a bit further*, Amelia thought, crossing her fingers tightly, trying to will the cat into the basket. *A little further now …*

Sam was waving a hand under his nose, and Amelia realised what was going to happen. *Oh no!*

"*Ahhhh-chooo!*" Sam sneezed. It was even louder than the sound of builders coming from outside. The cat froze, puffing her tail out. Then she shot up a stack of hay bales, leaping gracefully from them on to the old beams that supported the roof. She darted up them, climbing ever higher.

"All this hay got up my nose," said Sam, sniffing as he gazed around. "I'm really sorry."

The cat was crouched on the highest beam, peering down at them. There

was no way either Sam or Amelia
could climb up that far. It was much
too dangerous – if they fell they would
get hurt. Every now and again, the cat
bunched up the muscles in her legs as if
she was about to jump, but
then remained still.

"She'll be OK,
won't she?" said Sam
anxiously. "I thought cats
liked being up high?"

"They do," said
Amelia, nodding.

"But she's *really* high up ..."

A jolt of worry passed through her.

"Sam, I think she's stuck!"

CHAPTER EIGHT

Sam sprinted out of the barn to fetch
Mr Stevens.

"Don't jump," Amelia said in
desperation as the cat meowed and flicked
her tail from side to side. "Please don't
jump down!"

Mr Stevens came hurrying into the barn

with Sam. "Poor cat!" he said. "I don't think I've got a ladder long enough to reach up there."

Amelia remembered something she'd seen in the yard outside. "What about that forklift truck? If we stacked the bales high enough, she might climb down them on her own."

A few minutes later, Amelia and Sam were watching anxiously as the farmer drove the forklift inside, and began to manoeuvre the bales into position. They set the cat carrier with the tuna on the floor, and left the cat alone in the barn.

"I hope this works," said Sam, his eyes pressed up against the door, which they left open a crack. At his side, Amelia watched too, with her heart in her mouth.

The tortoiseshell waited for a few minutes, then suddenly leapt, her paws outstretched, and landed perfectly on the topmost bale. Amelia shared a glance of excitement with Sam. She wanted to cheer, but she didn't want to risk scaring the cat off again. Lightly, the cat jumped from bale to bale, until she reached the cat basket. She stretched up and peered inside. Then, with one graceful leap, she jumped in.

Amelia darted into the barn and shut the basket's door. The mother cat hissed and clawed angrily when she realised she was trapped. Through the slats of the door, Amelia saw her wild, flashing eyes, and she wished she could comfort the frightened animal.

"It's OK," she said soothingly. "We're taking you to see your kittens."

"Quick thinking," Mr Stevens said with a grin, as Amelia whooped and high-fived Sam. "Her kittens will be pleased to see her, I reckon."

Amelia's happiness dimmed. The
mother cat had been away from her
kittens for almost twenty-four hours
now. What if they smelled like people?
Would she accept them back? *Please*, she
thought. *Please let us not be too late.*

At Animal Ark, Mrs Hope carefully lifted
the cat out of the basket. She hissed and
swatted at the vet with her claws, but then
she crouched on the consulting-room
table and let the Hopes check her over.
Amelia's mum and gran had dropped the
kittens off at the surgery, and they were
back in the cosy incubator.

Waiting for the vets' verdict, Amelia
realised she was biting her fingernails.
In the background, Mr Stevens grasped
his cap in both hands.

"She's thin, and she's got a cut on her
paw," said Mr Hope at last, straightening
up. "But other than that, she's in good
health." He dabbed a liquid on the back

of the cat's neck. "Flea treatment," he explained. "We'll give her a worming tablet too."

Relief coursed through Amelia. The cat meowed restlessly while Mrs Hope scanned her with the microchip reader that Mandy had used on Mac.

"No chip," Mrs Hope confirmed.

"She must be a stray," said Amelia.

"From the look of her fur, I'd agree," said Mrs Hope. "Come on then, my love. Time to put you back with your kittens."

Mr Hope removed the incubator's lid and Mrs Hope slipped the cat inside. The cat stood for a moment, looking uncertain as the kittens cried. She approached them, then stopped and stared. Her ears were pricked forwards. Another step.

Amelia exchanged an agonised glance with Sam. What if they had handled the kittens too much and their mother rejected them? After everything that had

happened, it couldn't go wrong now!

The cat slowly put out her pink tongue and licked first the ginger kitten and then the three tortoiseshells. For the first time since Amelia had seen her, she seemed to relax completely, lying down and blinking her eyes. At once the kittens snuggled up to her, nudged at her belly and started suckling her milk. Even through the glass, Amelia could hear the mother cat purring. She looked at Sam and saw a grin on his face, like the one she could feel on her own.

Mr Stevens settled his cap back on his head with a broad smile. "I'd really like to adopt the cat and take her home with me," he said. "I feel bad for not realising she was a stray. She'll keep the mice in check around the farm."

"Are you sure? She may not want to live in the farmhouse," Mrs Hope warned him, as she washed her hands at the sink. "Stray cats often like to keep their independence."

"Well," said Mr Stevens, "she can stay in the barn if she prefers. Either way, I'll make sure she's fed."

"Her kittens need to be with her for another eight weeks," Mr Hope said. "Then you can collect her."

Mr Stevens stroked the largest tortoiseshell kitten, whose tail had a

white tip. She nuzzled
his finger and he
laughed. "This one
seems to like me,"
he said. "I think
I'll adopt her
as well."

Amelia was delighted.
"What about the other
kittens?" she asked. "Can they live on the
farm too?"

But Mr Stevens shook his head. "I can't
look after five cats, I'm afraid."

"Oh," said Sam, his shoulders drooping.

Poor kittens, thought Amelia. She looked
to the incubator, where they had curled

up against their mother's soft tummy,
kneading the fur with their little paws.
The ginger kitten had a splash of milk
on his nose. He licked it off with his tiny
pink tongue. *Mr and Mrs Hope don't think
I'm responsible enough to help out here*, she
thought. *Well, I'm going to show them that I
am – because I'm going to help the kittens!*

She turned to Mr and Mrs Hope.

"We'll find homes for them," she said.
"Won't we, Sam?"

Sam stared at her for a moment, and
then he grinned. "Definitely!" he said.

Mrs Hope looked thoughtful. "There's
no harm in letting them try, is there?"
she said to her husband.

Mr Hope agreed. "All right, then.
You two can have a go at finding them
homes. But let us know if you get stuck."

"We will," said Amelia. "But we'll
do it – I promise!" *And then*, she thought
to herself, *Mr and Mrs Hope will have to see
that I can help out at Animal Ark, won't they?*

As the Hopes began getting ready for
their next patient, Amelia asked Sam,

133

"Do you want to come round for tea? We can talk about finding homes for the kittens. And you've got to try one of Mum's salted caramel cupcakes — they taste amazing."

"Cool!" said Sam. "That would be really brilliant."

"Caramel," said Mr Stevens thoughtfully. "The mother cat has got lots of caramel shades in her fur, hasn't she? That would be a good name for her."

"Yes!" agreed Amelia and Sam.

"Then Caramel it is," said Mr Stevens. "And what about the kitten?"

Amelia pointed to the white tip on her tail. "Snowdrop?" she suggested.

"Perfect," said Mr Stevens, and everyone smiled.

Amelia and Sam decided to walk back to the B&B first to fetch Mac. Side by side they set off up the lane into the village. The ducks were on the pond again, and the breeze ruffled the reeds by the water's edge. A pair of butterflies danced overhead.

Amelia found herself humming. She had a feeling she was going to love Welford as much as York. Maybe even

more! She'd already made so many friends – both animals and people. Even the thought of starting her new school next week felt less frightening. *Welford doesn't quite feel like home yet*, she thought, *but it's starting to.*

At the B&B, Sam fetched Mac's lead, and he and Amelia walked the puppy to Amelia's house. In the lane, Mac peed on a patch of grass on the verge.

"Good boy!" Sam said, ruffling Mac's head and giving him a treat. "He really is learning!" He knelt down to hug him. "Maybe I'll be able to keep this little guy after all."

"I really hope so," said Amelia.

She felt a rush of happiness as she wondered what other animals she was going to meet at Animal Ark, and what adventures she and Sam would have next.

I can't wait to find out!

The End

Read on for a sneak peek at
Amelia and Sam's next adventure!

ANiMAL ARK

Bunny Trouble
Lucy Daniels

Izzy turned and gave a yelp of delight.
Amelia handed her Tulip, and Izzy buried
her face in the rabbit's fur. "Oh, Tulip!
Don't ever run away again!"

Sam was grinning. "Now we just need
to sneak back out!"

"WOOF!"

They all spun towards the sound.
The hedge rattled. The nettles quaked.
And Mac burst out of the grass, his lead
trailing behind him.

"Mac, no!" cried Sam, his brown eyes
wide with panic.

But instead of running to Sam, the puppy headed straight for the house. Amelia's stomach flipped over. Mrs Cranbourne would see them!

They gave chase. Brambles snagged their clothes, but they didn't stop until they'd caught up with Mac. He'd reached the back of the house. There was a cat flap in the door, and to Amelia's horror, the puppy rammed his nose against it. Mac bounced back on to the doormat with a howl of surprise. He lay there shaking his head. Amelia almost laughed.

Then the door flew open. Mrs Cranbourne stood in the doorway, hands on hips. Her face was red with fury.

"What are you doing in my garden?" she shouted. She stared at Amelia and Sam, and then she turned to Izzy. Her eyes dropped to Tulip, with her juice-stained fur, and she drew in a sharp breath.

"So that's who's been eating my strawberries!" Mrs Cranbourne shouted. Amelia opened her mouth to explain, but Mrs Cranbourne took a threatening step towards Izzy and Tulip. "THIEF!"

Amelia knew they had to escape. "Run!" she cried.

Read **Bunny Trouble** to find out what happens next ...

Animal Advice

Do you love animals as much as Amelia and
Sam? Here are some tips on how to look after
them from veterinary surgeon Sarah McGurk.

Caring for your pet

1 Animals need clean water at all times.

2 They need to be fed too – ask your vet what kind of
   food is best, and how much the animal needs.

3 Some animals, such as dogs, need exercise every day.

4 Animals also need lots of love. You should always
   be very gentle with your pets and be careful not to do
   anything that might hurt them.

When to go to the vet

Sometimes animals get ill. Like you, they will mostly get better on their own. But if your pet has hurt itself or seems very unwell, then a trip to the vet might be needed. Some pets also need to be vaccinated, to prevent them from getting dangerous diseases. Your vet can tell you what your pet needs.

Helping wildlife

1 Always ask an adult before you go near any animals you don't know.

2 If you find an animal or bird which is injured or can't move, it is best not to touch it.

3 If you are worried, you can phone an animal charity such as the RSPCA (SSPCA in Scotland) for help.

Where **animals** need you!

COLLECT ALL OF AMELIA AND SAM'S EXCITING ADVENTURES!

www.animalark.co.uk

🐾 Discover all the books in the series

🐾 Read exciting extracts

🐾 Find fun downloads

🐾 And lots more!